# WELCOME TO

Collect the special coins in this book.
You will earn one gold coin for
every chapter you read.

Once you have finished all the chapters,
find out what to do with your gold coins at
the back of the book.

With special thanks to Michael Ford

*To the "hopping lot"*

And with extra special thanks to Toby Cook

www.beastquest.co.uk

ORCHARD BOOKS

First published in Great Britain in 2013 by Orchard Books
This edition published in 2017 by The Watts Publishing Group

7 9 10 8

Text © 2013 Beast Quest Limited.
Cover and inside illustrations by Steve Sims
© Beast Quest Limited 2013

Beast Quest is a registered trademark of Beast Quest Limited
Series created by Beast Quest Limited, London

A CIP catalogue record for this book is available from the British Library.

ISBN 978 1 40832 408 0

Printed in Great Britain by Clays Ltd, Elcograf S.p.A.

The paper and board used in this book are made from wood from responsible sources

Orchard Books
An imprint of Hachette Children's Group
Part of The Watts Publishing Group Limited
Carmelite House, 50 Victoria Embankment, London EC4Y 0DZ

An Hachette UK Company
www.hachette.co.uk
www.hachettechildrens.co.uk

# VIKTOR
## THE DEADLY ARCHER

BY ADAM BLADE

ORCHARD

# CONTENTS

# STORY ONE

I've never known a summer like this in Avantia. The ground bakes under the sun's glare and leaves turn brown on the trees.

Since my magic has been taken by the Wizard Court, books are all that I have left. I stare into my crystal ball but its surface is dark. I feel more like an old man every day. Perhaps it is time for me to live out my days as a hermit.

But what's this? A strange feeling creeps over me. It seems I still have one power left – the ability to sense evil in Avantia. An ancient malice has returned! A Beast has arrived and I am powerless to help.

Yours, in gravest times,

Aduro, a wizard no more

# A KINGDOM
# AFLAME

Tom rested a hand on the cool stone wall and leaned out of his turret window. A bead of sweat trickled down his cheek. He brushed it away.

"So hot…" he muttered. "Not a breath of wind for days."

The air was like thick soup, and heat shimmered over the battlements of King Hugo's castle. All of the windows had been thrown open. Courtiers fanned themselves as they went about their duties, and servants scurried from one spot of shade to the next. The sun glared down like a giant burning eye, relentless in a sky without even a shred of cloud.

Tom wiped his brow and let his eyes travel across the parched Avantian landscape beyond the castle battlements. Somewhere out there, his enemies waited. Kensa the Witch, once banished but now returned, and Sanpao the King of the Makai pirates. Tom felt his hands ball into fists. *This heatwave has something to do with Kensa's magic, I'm sure*, he thought.

Riders had brought reports of

cracks opening in the dry meadows and swallowing whole herds of cattle. In the north, ice was melting off the frozen plains and threatened to flood the nearby towns. Here in the city though, the wells were almost dry.

A shape below caught Tom's eye. It was Aduro, still dressed in his heavy purple robes, despite the heat. He was shuffling across the courtyard, bent over with age now that the Circle of Wizards had stripped him of his magical powers.

Aduro glanced up and saw Tom. "Hail, young warrior," he called. "I must speak with you. Something is afoot in Avantia. Meet me in the Wizard's Chamber."

*A new Quest?* Tom wondered.

He changed into a clean tunic, then went to the chest at the end of his bed, taking out his shield and newly sharpened sword. Dashing from his chamber, he crossed the corridor to Elenna's room and thumped on the door. "Hurry," he said. "Aduro has news."

Elenna opened the door. Her hair was stuck to her temples with the heat, but she was already clutching her bow, with her quiver looped over her shoulder. Silver stood behind her, yawning. "Good," Elenna said. "I'm tired of sitting around."

They crossed a gallery and took another set of spiral stairs to the Wizard's Chamber at the top of the castle. Bursting through the door, they found not Aduro, but Daltec. He was lying back on a bed, and sat bolt upright when he saw them.

"What are you doing?" said Elenna.

Daltec gave a sheepish grin. "Just working on a new spell," he said.

"It didn't look like it," said Tom. "It

looked like you were taking a nap."

Daltec stood up and Tom saw that the straw-filled mattress was glowing slightly blue. "Try it out," said the young apprentice, waving a hand over the bed.

Tom frowned. "We don't have time for this. Aduro's coming."

"But he's not here yet," said Daltec. "Just try it."

Tom sighed, and lowered himself onto the bed. Almost at once, a cool sensation spread over his skin. It was like lying in a mountain stream. He couldn't help the gasp of delight that escaped his lips.

"My turn," said Elenna, hopping on beside him. "Oh! It's wonderful!"

Daltec puffed out his chest proudly.

"I should be able to cast the spell over every bed in the castle," he said.

A shuffling sound on the stairs made them all turn. Aduro was leaning against the wall, breathing heavily.

*Of course*, thought Tom. *He can't magic himself up the stairs any more.*

Tom rushed forward and helped his ashen-faced mentor into the chamber. They sat him down on the magic bed, but he didn't seem to notice the cooling spell. Daltec fetched a cup, and with a click of his fingers it filled to the brim with water.

Tom smiled. *His magic is getting better by the day.*

Aduro sipped from the cup and wiped droplets of water from his grey beard. "I have to warn you," he croaked. "Evil is coming."

"Kensa and Sanpao?" Tom said.

Aduro shook his head. "No. It feels…ancient. A Beast."

Tom's hand fell to his sword. "Whatever it is, we're ready."

Aduro gave a weak smile. "I knew you would be," he said. "Daltec, consult the magic ball as I've shown you."

The young wizard looked suddenly serious as he approached the plinth in the centre of the room. Aduro's crystal ball sat on top on a cushion. Daltec raised his hands on either side, and muttered a few words. Colours swirled within the depths of the orb.

"What can you see?" asked Aduro urgently.

A frown creased Daltec's brow. He stepped back. "A golden arrow," he mumbled. "What could it mean?"

Aduro stood up. "What else can you see?" he asked, his voice trembling.

Daltec approached the ball again and raised his hands. "I see the Golden Armour," he said. His face paled, and he clutched his temples with a grimace. He sank to his knees and the crystal ball darkened again.

Elenna rushed to Daltec's side, and helped him to stand. "What happened?"

Aduro placed his gnarled hand on the crystal ball, stroking it lovingly. "It's just the power of the magic," he said. "He will recover soon."

"But what did the vision mean?" said Tom.

Aduro turned to him, his old eyes watery in his lined face. "It means the Golden Armour is in danger," he said. "We must get to the Armoury!"

1

# AN ANCIENT TERROR RETURNS

As Tom and Elenna started for the door, Aduro tried to follow. Daltec placed a hand on his shoulder. "No, master, you must rest here."

Aduro nodded, and Tom took the stairs three at a time. He heard the shuffle of Elenna's feet and Silver's panting close behind. Aduro's expression lingered in his mind's eye – a mixture of fear and disbelief.

*What will I find at the Armoury?*

Tom sprinted across the courtyard under the burning glare of the sun, and climbed down the steps towards the armoury beneath the castle's main hall. "Wait outside," he said to Elenna.

He drew his sword as he pressed down the narrow passage. Torches blazed on the stone walls. The door to the armoury was open, and Tom crossed the threshold into the cool chamber.

There was no Beast here. The Master of Arms was whistling a merry tune as he polished the panels of the Golden Armour.

"Oh!" he said, looking surprised. "Greetings, Master Tom. I wasn't expecting you."

Tom stopped, letting the cool air settle on his skin. "Is everything all right?" he asked.

"Everything but this devilish heat," said the Master of Arms. "Never

known anything like it in all my days."

Tom allowed himself to relax. *Perhaps Aduro was wrong. Maybe there's no threat to Avantia at all...*

His eyes travelled over the scratched and dented golden plates. The suit of armour had once belonged to his father, Taladon, and now it had passed to him. The Master of the Beasts did not have to wear the separate sections – their magical powers stayed with him whenever the suit was safely in the armoury. Tom stroked the breastplate, and felt the magic flowing beneath his fingers. *I'll never let it come to harm.*

Just then, a wild squeaking erupted from the doorway and a ferret scurried into the chamber. Its eyes were wide with alarm as it clambered up the Master of Arms's leg and on to his shoulder.

"What's the matter, Slinky?" asked the man.

The ferret nuzzled his neck, still squeaking.

A scream from outside cut through the air, and Tom's head jerked around.

"Tom!" called Elenna. "Come quickly."

Tom rushed back up the passage and skidded to a halt at the entrance. Across the top of the battlements over the palace gate soldiers were aiming their crossbows at something. More soldiers were rushing from either side. Their shouts carried down:

"What is it?"

"Call more men!"

"Stop there, foe!"

The Master of Arms emerged at the top of the steps beside Tom, his ferret clutched in his arms. "Is the castle being attacked?" he asked.

A flash of gold caught Tom's eye and, in the same instant, the Master of Arms flew backwards. His ferret leapt from his hands. A golden arrow as tall as a man and thick as a sapling was sticking through his chest, pinning him to the Armoury door.

His face was creased in confusion and pain, but no blood seeped from the wound. The ferret shot across the courtyard and into the stable.

The Master of Arms's mouth gaped open as he tried to speak. Then his head sank back.

"Is he dead? asked Elenna.

Tom felt his wrist. There was a softly beating pulse. "No." There was still no bleeding from the wound. "I don't understand…"

"There's no reason you should," said a croaking voice. Tom glanced up to see Aduro standing nearby, with Daltec at his side. "He is not dead." The former wizard paused. "His fate is far worse."

The shouts on the battlements rose in pitch. "Stop him!"

Tom heard the pounding of hooves. It sounded like an army riding towards the castle. Aduro stared at the castle walls. There was another sound too – a hollow knocking,

like someone banging wooden poles together. Then the soldiers on the walls ducked behind their defences.

A horse as tall as a building leapt over the gate towers, and landed with a crash in the middle of the courtyard.

It wasn't the creature's size that made
Tom's heart freeze in his chest. The
horse's body was like a scaffold of
pale, fleshless bone – a living, moving
skeleton, shifting on white hooves.
His black nostrils gaped wide as he

gave a mighty snort.

"That's impossible," gasped Elenna, frozen to the spot beside Tom.

A rider sat astride the massive steed – a hideous knight at least ten feet tall, wearing leather trousers. Two horns thrust from his ridged helmet. In his hand he clutched a gleaming golden bow. The knight's feet rested in stirrups either side of his stallion's great curved belly of heaving white ribs. He gripped the leather reins that looped over the snow-white skull and yanked the horse's head around. The empty eye-sockets flashed at Tom. Even the horse's tail was a short row of clicking bones, whipping the air.

"What are you...?" muttered Tom.

The rider didn't speak. He kicked his

steed's flanks and lunged forwards. The horse's bones ground together in a way that made Tom's stomach twist.

Tom drew his sword and levelled its point at the terrible new enemy. "You won't go any further," he said. "Not while there's blood in my veins."

A hissing cackle came from the knight's mouth. The horse's skull tossed angrily. As the rider trotted towards him, he twisted round to reach over his back. Tom saw now where the golden arrow had come from. Down his spine bristled three more, like golden spikes.

"Where is the Golden Armour?" growled the knight.

"I'll never tell you," said Tom.

The knight shook his head as he

snapped one of the arrows off and
placed it across his bow-string. He
aimed the shaft straight between

Tom's eyes, and drew back the enormous longbow.

"Then you will die," he said.

# THE DEADLY
# HUNTSMAN

The arrow scorched through the air like a shaft of fire. Tom dived sideways, feeling it whip past his head as he rolled to safety. Scrambling to his feet again, he saw the rider steer his horse alongside the hanging body of the Master of Arms. Leaning from the saddle, the knight seized the arrow pinning the helpless man to the door.

Golden light crackled over the arrow shaft.

"What are you doing to him?" shouted Elenna. She was sheltering behind a water trough, and drew an arrow from her own quiver. Tom saw the Master's eyes open, then roll back in his head. The arrow disappeared from his body like fading mist, then magically reappeared on the knight's back. The man sank to the ground, groaning.

*Can Aduro be right?* Tom wondered. *Can he still be alive?*

The knight retrieved the second arrow, sweeping it up in his hand. Then he spurred his skeleton horse hard. The wretched animal rose on its hind legs, its joints knocking horribly.

Tom leapt back, shielding his face

from the wheeling hooves, and fell down with a cry. The horse tore into the Armoury entrance, showering dust, then galloped into the passage beyond with its rider huddled close to its bony neck.

"No!"Tom cried, but he was too late. The huge knight emerged once more, hoisting the Golden Breastplate over his head in triumph, as easily as if it weighed nothing.

An arrow sped past, but simply rattled through the stallion's frame. Tom saw Elenna put another arrow shaft in her bow, aiming it higher. Tom shook his head at her.

*We need to understand this Beast before we can fight it*, he thought.

Elenna lowered her bow, clearly

seeing what he was thinking.

The knight laid the breastplate across the front of his saddle, and glanced around the courtyard. His eyes, black as coal, settled on Aduro. The former wizard stood his ground.

"How did you get free?" asked Aduro, his voice shaking.

*Aduro knows him*, Tom realised.

The knight snarled and his horse started towards Aduro, who fell backwards, landing heavily. "That is not important," said the knight. "Now I have a little protection, it's time for me to go hunting."

With a wild roar, he spurred his stallion into a thundering gallop across the courtyard. Instead of leaping the walls, he charged straight towards the raised drawbridge, scattering the soldiers who guarded it. With an almighty crash of splintering wood, the drawbridge exploded

outwards, and he vaulted the moat in a single bound. Soon his pounding hooves were like distant thunder. Elenna came out from behind the water trough and Daltec rushed to Aduro's side. "Are you hurt?" he asked.

Aduro stood weakly and shook his head. "It's not me you should worry about," he said. "The Good Beasts of Avantia are in danger."

A tingle of dread chilled Tom's blood. *The knight is a Beast hunter?*

"See to the Master of Arms," said Aduro to Daltec. "Magic him to the infirmary at once."

Tom stood over the man's body. His ferret had emerged and was sniffing at his motionless fingers. The man's skin looked grey and wasted. Tom placed a hand over his parted lips and felt the soft warmth of slow breathing. "I don't understand," he said. "That arrow should have killed him for certain."

Aduro nodded. "If it were any ordinary arrow, it surely would have.

But these arrows are magical. They suck the life-force from their victims, leaving the body as a mindless husk."

Daltec waved his hands over the stricken man and muttered a spell. Within moments, the Master of Arms had vanished.

"Will he ever get better?" Tom asked.

Aduro turned and walked towards the stairs that led to his chamber. "Follow me," he said over his shoulder. "I need to check something."

"Let me help," called Daltec. He waved a hand and the courtyard vanished.

Tom found himself back in the Wizard's Chamber, with the others at his side. Aduro was already searching through books on his shelves with his fingertips. "It's got to be here somewhere," he growled. Then he clicked his fingers. "Oh, I forgot…"

He leant over the side of his oak desk, and pressed a finger under the rim. Tom heard a click and a secret drawer slid out. Inside was an ancient-looking book bound in

cracked red leather. Gold lettering spelled out a title.

"*Annals of the Archers,*" Elenna read.

As Aduro placed the book on the desk, Tom's fingers played over the hilt of his sword.

"We can't afford to delay any longer," he said. "That thing might be attacking one of the Good Beasts already. If he sucks their life-force away too, he'll become unstoppable."

Aduro creaked open the book and turned quickly through the brown pages. "I never thought I'd need to consult this," he said. "It is my master's chronicle. We thought the kingdom had seen the last of…" He gasped, his finger falling on the page.

Tom leaned past Aduro and read the title of the page in spidery, faded script: "'Viktor, the Deadly Archer.' Is that the knight's name?"

Aduro nodded dumbly, eyes flashing over the text. "But Viktor should not be here," he said. "It's...*impossible*!"

# 4

# HUNTING THE HUNTER

"I've never heard of him before," said Tom.

"Few people have," Aduro said. "Viktor has not ridden the plains of Avantia since the times of your great-great-grandfather. He was the last of the Deadly Archers, and by far the most wicked. These hunters travelled from kingdom to kingdom, killing

Beasts for sport."

"That's terrible!" said Elenna, her hand flying to her mouth.

"The Circle of Wizards dealt with all the Archers, imprisoning them in the Chamber of Pain."

Tom shuddered, remembering the terrible island prison from his battle with Grashkor the Beast Guard. "But it's impossible to escape the Chamber of Pain."

Aduro raised an eyebrow. "Viktor was not locked up in the Chamber," he said. "The Wizards did not want to take any chances, so they buried him beneath a thick layer of ice in the kingdom's north. There could have been no escape from there."

"But there was," said Daltec,

quietly. "Tell me, Master, how can I stop Viktor?"

Aduro placed a gnarled hand on his shoulder. "Your magic is not powerful enough yet, my brave apprentice," he said. "I fear no one can defeat the black knight. Perhaps the combined power of the Circle of Wizards…"

"Then call on them," said Elenna.

Aduro shook his head. "I cannot. I am no longer one of the Circle. And Daltec will only become part of it once he has completed his training."

Elenna brought her fist down onto the table. "We can't rest here while the kingdom suffers," she said.

"She's right," said Tom. "If the Wizards won't fight Viktor, then we must!"

Aduro read on for a moment. He closed the book swiftly, and took a step back from the desk, a haunted, distant expression on his face.

"What is it?" asked Tom.

Aduro took a deep breath, then placed a gnarled hand on Tom's shoulder. "Your courage does you great credit, but I have just learned a deadly secret about this Beast. A secret that you must know, too."

Tom took a deep breath to calm his nerves. "What is it?"

"Viktor once stole the life-force from a Master of the Beasts. He could do the same again."

A spark of doubt caught in Tom's heart. Not only was Viktor a deadly Beast, he had stolen the courage of a

Master for himself!

*But if I ran from every threat, Avantia would have been destroyed long ago...*

"So if one of Viktor's arrows pierced Tom..." Elenna began.

"...the black knight would take Tom's life-force," Daltec finished.

Tom sank on to a stool, his head in his hands. "This has to be Kensa's doing," he said. "She must have sent this heatwave to melt the ice and free Viktor to hunt Good Beasts and to steal my life-force." Tom felt rage burn through him. "If I had not failed in my attempts to defeat Kensa before now—"

Elenna stood before him. "Don't waste time blaming yourself," she said. "We have a Quest to complete."

His friend's words brought a sliver of hope. "Let's saddle Storm and ride," Tom said. "Viktor beat one Master of the Beasts, but this one will not fall to him."

Tom led Storm out of the stables, with Elenna and Silver at his side. Across the courtyard, carpenters were already at work on repairs to the drawbridge, and masons were gathered around the ruined armoury.

*I'll be without the power of the Golden Breastplate*, thought Tom. *This Quest is the deadliest yet.*

Daltec approached, looking grave, with the *Annals of the Archers* tucked

under his arm. "Be careful," he told
them. "Don't take any risks."

Tom raised an eyebrow. How could
he defeat a Beast like Viktor without

putting his life on the line?

"Don't worry," said Tom, swinging a leg over Storm's back. He helped Elenna up behind him, then took the reins in his hands.

"Wait a moment!" said Daltec. "You'll need a map to help you find Viktor." The young Wizard took the book from under his arm, and opened it to the last page. Tucked inside the cover was a folded piece of parchment. He blew on it, and it floated through the air into Tom's hands. Daltec smiled shyly. "Another little trick of mine," he explained. "Easy, really."

Tom unfolded the ancient parchment gently. As he did, it began to glow a soft golden colour. Across

its surface was drawn a crude map of the kingdom. A golden dot, no bigger than a fly, moved slowly across the parchment.

"The map will show you where the Deadly Archer is at all times," said Daltec. "Keep it close to you."

The dot was heading north, and had almost reached the Forest of Fear.

"He's going towards the Northern Mountains," said Elenna. "It must be Arcta that he's hunting."

Tom swallowed as he thought of the magnificent Good Beast, guarding the jagged peaks. He imagined a golden arrow piercing Arcta's body. *If anything happens to the Mountain Giant, I won't be able to forgive myself.*

"Ready for a new Quest?" he said to Elenna.

"Let's ride out!" she said.

Tom nudged Storm's flanks. The stallion whinnied and cantered towards the remains of the drawbridge with Silver at his side. As they picked up speed to a gallop, Tom heaved on the reins. Storm leapt the moat, landing with a bone-shaking thump on the other side. Silver almost fell, but scrambled up the bank.

Tom wheeled Storm around and noticed Aduro's purple cloak as he watched from the courtyard within. The old wizard raised his hand in farewell.

Tom raised his own hand in reply.

As they galloped north, he wondered, *Will I ever see my old friend again?*

# 5

# FLYING FOES

Viktor's path was easy to follow
without the map. His horse's hooves
had torn up great clods of earth,
scarring the landscape. Fences were
broken in places where he'd galloped
mercilessly through. It was still hot,
but the sun didn't beat down as it
had before.

As they travelled, Tom gripped
the ruby jewel at his belt, seeking

any message from Arcta or the Good Beasts. Nothing. Dread weighed heavily on his shoulders. *What if the Deadly Archer reaches Arcta first? If he sucks out the Mountain Giant's spirit, he'll be unstoppable!*

Soon, they reached a farmhouse. Cattle in a nearby field were gathered in a huddle. "Something must have spooked them," said Elenna. "I think I can guess what."

A farmworker was leaning against a broken gate-post, while his wife tried to dab at his head with a damp cloth. He was bleeding from a cut under his hairline, and his arm was in a sling made from a torn piece of cloth. Tom slowed Storm as they approached.

"Please," said the frightened woman,

"don't hurt us!"

Tom held up a hand. "We mean no harm. What happened here?"

The man pointed a trembling finger northward. "A golden knight…" he said, "on a huge horse."

"A golden knight?" said Tom. So Viktor was already wearing the breastplate from the Golden Armour. Did that mean he'd possessed its strength of heart as well?

"That was one horrible horse," said the woman. "It had no flesh. It was like something out of a nightmare…"

Elenna slipped quickly from the saddle, and fished in Storm's saddlebag. She took out a pouch. "Stew these herbs in boiling water," she said. "Then drink the bitter liquid with some honey. It will help your wounds heal more quickly." She tossed the pouch over.

"Thank you!" the farmer's wife called as she caught it. "Be careful not to run into the knight!"

*That's exactly what I intend to do,* Tom thought, setting Storm off at a gallop. *We just need to find him first. At least now we know we're on the right track.*

As the day wore on, the sun dipped in the sky. Already it was cooler than it had been for days. "Kensa's spell is lifted, now that Viktor is freed," Tom said.

They lost track of Viktor's path in the long grasses south of the Forest of Fear, so Tom drew out the map. Storm was sweating, and dipped his head to drink from a trickling stream. The map showed a golden dot just inside the Forest of Fear itself.

"How strange," said Elenna. "There aren't any Beasts in the Forest. Why has Viktor stopped there?"

Tom frowned. "Perhaps he's tired."
His frown became a grin. "If he's
resting, it gives us time to catch him
up!"

Silver growled as a shadow passed
over them. Tom glanced up, expecting
to see a cloud.

But it was no cloud looming in the
sky. It was a great ship, the stained
timbers of its black hull encrusted
with moss and barnacles.

"Sanpao!" Tom gasped.

He quickly spurred Storm towards
a thicket of trees, and slid off the
horse's back. Had Sanpao's crew seen
them? No – they would have attacked
by now.

From the ship's masts, blood-red

flags were flying, all marked with
a Beast's skull – the emblem of the
Makai. Rigging clanked and flapped
in the breeze. Tom caught sight of
the Pirate King himself, his oiled
plait glistening as it dangled over his

broad, tattooed shoulders. He stood at the bow, leaning over the rail and pointing toward the Forest of Fear.

Silver let out a loud whine. Sanpao's head whipped round. Tom and Elenna ducked further into the thicket, and Elenna placed a hand on her wolf's head. "Hush, boy," she whispered.

Another figure stepped up behind Sanpao. It was Kensa.

"What is it?" she snapped. The Sorceress of Henkrall wore her long black cloak, covered in woven magical symbols.

Sanpao shook his head. "I thought I heard something," Tom heard him say.

Kensa clipped him around the back of the head. "What have I told you

about thinking? You let me do that,
bilge-breath." Her eyes roved over the
ship. "Can't this contraption of yours
go any faster? Get us to Laus!"

Sanpao glowered at Kensa, but
then turned to his men and bellowed,

"Tighten the mizzen, boys! I'll personally keel-haul anyone who idles!"

The pirate crew scurried across the deck, and winches screeched. The sails swelled further and the ship picked up speed.

"What's Laus?" asked Elenna.

"I don't know," said Tom, straightening up, "but we have to stop them."

"Leave it to me," said Elenna. She stepped out of their hiding place, and strung an arrow. She steadied herself and let the arrow fly, straight and true, slicing through one of the main ropes trailing from a spar. The mainsail flapped loose on one side, and Tom heard pirates curse as the ship

lurched and tipped. One almost fell over the deck-rail, but he managed to clamber back on board. As he did so, his eyes fell on Tom and Elenna.

"It's those wretched curs!" he said.

As the ship righted itself, Kensa ran to the stern and stared down with eyes hard as flint. Sanpao joined her, cutlass drawn. Elenna fired another arrow, and Sanpao jerked back as it lodged in the hull with a *thunk*.

"We know what you've done!" cried Tom. "You won't get away with it!"

"You can't stop us," yelled Kensa.

She grinned and drew back her arm. "Soon Laus will be ours."With a flash of her hand, she sent a bolt of lightning towards them. Tom and Elenna dived aside, but the fork smashed into the thicket of trees in an explosion of sparks. Fire spread

quickly over the plants around Storm and Silver. The animals leapt away in panic as the trees collapsed in a heap of ash.

The pirate ship shrank towards the horizon.

"What have I done?" asked Elenna. "They've escaped, and things are worse than ever."

"You tried your best," Tom reassured her as he mounted Storm again. "I want to know who Laus is. I thought the Beast was called Viktor."

He took out the map again, and saw that the golden dot hadn't moved from the Forest of Fear. Now though, he saw writing in the depths of the forest, pale silver and barely readable. He peered more closely. The letters spelled out 'Laus'.

"Are we chasing two Beasts now?" he said.

"Tom, look!" said Elenna. She was pointing to the charred remains of one of the trees. A whorl in the bark seemed to be swirling. It formed into the shape of Daltec's face. His lips were moving and gradually they heard the whisper of his voice.

"...don't have much time," he was saying, "My magic is weak. Laus is a Beast of the forest. He only appears when the two strongest stags lock in battle." His image began to fade and his voice cracked. "Must be protected..." he said. "...can be turned to Evil... Viktor powerful..."

The face disappeared, leaving only

blackened bark. "So Viktor isn't after Arcta at all," said Elenna. "He wants the Beast called Laus."

Tom turned northward. Sanpao's ship was just a dot, like a distant bird, and the Forest of Fear was a smudge on the horizon. A savage pirate and a cunning Witch…and two Beasts to face…

*This Quest just became more dangerous than ever*, he thought.

# 6

# THE FOREST BEAST

Tom leapt on to Storm's back, and
Elenna scrambled up behind him.
"To the Forest!" Tom cried, and gave
Storm a nudge with his heel. The
stallion took off at a gallop, with
Silver racing alongside.

"If only I hadn't been resting at the
palace," Tom said. "I should have been
scouring the kingdom to find Kensa."

"Don't blame yourself," said Elenna,

over the thunder of Storm's hooves. "You can't be everywhere at once."

As they approached the fringes of the forest, daylight faded. A full moon rose above the landscape, casting an eerie glow. Tom slowed Storm and they entered the trees. Through the branches there was no sign of Sanpao's ship.

Following Viktor's path wasn't hard. Bushes torn up from their roots littered the ground, and snapped branches hung down. *I hope we're in time*, thought Tom.

Storm stalled and whinnied in panic, and Tom gripped his sword hilt. But the forest around them was silent.

"What is it, boy?" Tom whispered, laying a hand on Storm's mane.

The stallion stepped sideways, and Tom saw his hooves splashing at the edge of a marsh. A smell of rotten eggs rose from the putrid pond, and flies buzzed over the algae-covered surface. In the centre of the swamp, bubbles rose and burst into a froth.

"There must be some sort of crack at the floor of the pond," said Elenna. "That's where the bubbles are coming from."

Tom shuddered. "And we almost walked right into—"

He froze at the sound of a crash and the splinter of branches. Then there was a strange bellowing. It could only be...

"Viktor!" whispered Elenna, her eyes wide and face pale.

Tom steered Storm away from the marsh in the direction of the sound, glad to get away from the stench of the pond. He heard another sound like wood knocking against wood, and heaving breaths. *Is that the skeleton horse?*

They emerged at the edge of a clearing, but it wasn't Viktor who stood before them. Two proud stags, their brown coats glistening with sweat in the moonlight, were fighting. Their giant antlers tangled as they lunged and parried head-first. They parted and leapt forward again with a mighty crash, nostrils snorting and eyes rolling wildly.

Tom remembered Daltec's words: *He only appears when the two*

*strongest stags lock in battle.*

"We're about to see a new Beast," Tom whispered to Elenna. His friend's mouth had dropped open in astonishment.

Both stags reared up, fore-hooves wheeling. Then they fell towards each other. As their antlers clashed, splinters of blinding light shot out.

A strange keening sound erupted from the throat of the stags. Tom's heart skipped a beat. Where there had been two creatures, now there was only one. A single stag with two heads, each sprouting a set of branching silver antlers. The Beast's fur-matted body rippled with muscle, and its silver hooves scoured the undergrowth. None of its four tiny red eyes seemed to have spotted them yet.

Tom marvelled at the creature, but his awe was tinged with dread. He could see how powerful Laus was, from his muscles and huge size. If Viktor was to pierce Laus with one of his soul-sucking arrows, his strength would be unimaginable.

Laus tossed his heads and bellowed so loud that the leaves of the trees shook.

*Oh no!* thought Tom. *Viktor will surely hear that...*

Tom touched the ruby lodged in his belt. It gave him the power to communicate with Beasts, and he needed to keep Laus quiet.

*Calm,* Tom said with his mind. *There's no danger here...*

The Stag Beast paused for a moment, then swung its massive heads around. The beady red eyes glinted with rage and it bellowed again. There was something evil in the Beast's eyes – those two noble creatures had been transformed into something wicked. With a leap, it charged at them across the clearing.

*No! We're here to protect you!*

But Laus didn't seem to hear Tom's messages. He tossed his double antlers, and Tom just had time to bring his shield around. The blow flung him sideways into Elenna and they both rolled across the ground. "Keep out of the way!"Tom shouted to his friend, climbing to his feet and drawing his sword.

As Laus launched himself again, Tom parried with his sword. Metal rang out against horn as they clashed. It was like facing a swordsman with countless blades. Tom thrust with his shield and staggered backwards, trying desperately to stand his ground. Moonlight glinted off the

silvered antlers, casting shards of
vicious light that made Tom's eyes
water.

He heard the twang of Elenna's
bowstring and the Beast backed off as
an arrow sped past. Another followed,
and Laus jerked sideways. Tom
realised his friend was trying to keep

the two-headed stag at bay, rather than harm it. Silver joined the fight too, yapping and snarling around the Beast's stamping hooves.

Tom managed to advance a few steps, battering Laus back with his shield. The Beast's breaths were hot and heavy. *He's tiring*, Tom thought.

"Keep fighting!" he called to Elenna. "We can defeat him!"

Then he heard Elenna gasp, and the sudden chilling clatter of bones. Abandoning his assault, he glanced back. Viktor was at the other side of the clearing, mounted on his skeleton horse. His breastplate shone gold, with the arrows bristling at his back. Tom burned with fury, and he pointed his sword at the Deadly Archer with

all his bravery.

"That belongs to me!" he said.

Viktor raised the visor of his horned black helmet, and laughed. He reached behind him, to his belt scabbard, and drew out a blade of blackened iron as long as a man.

"I'll enjoy killing you," he snarled.

Tom looked back and saw Laus lurking in the trees. There was only one way to save the Stag Beast, and that was to defeat Viktor. He stepped into the centre of the clearing.

"Dismount, Viktor," he said, sending out a challenge. "Let's see how good a swordsman you really are."

1

# DESPERATE TIMES

Viktor laid a hand on his skeleton horse's neck and muttered, "Sleep, Ossator!"

The stallion gave a strange hollow whinny. The bones of its body collapsed in on themselves, falling into a heap on the ground and leaving Viktor standing. He stepped away from the remains of his steed.

Tom staggered back, astonished.

"You're impressed by my little trick, I see," said Viktor.

The cruel knight swished his sword from side to side in a blur that made Tom dizzy. He suddenly felt very small as Viktor stamped towards him. *How can I face this enemy? He's bigger, more powerful, and he has the strength of heart from the stolen breastplate!*

Viktor lunged, lightning quick, and Tom side-stepped. Sparks flew from their clashing blades.

"You're fast," said Viktor. "But not fast enough. You'll see."

Tom tried a slash of his own, following up with cuts, stabs and feints. Viktor knocked every strike aside, almost casually. The Deadly Archer sighed, as if bored, then swung his weapon, catching Tom's shield and sending him crashing to the ground.

As he shook his spinning head, Tom saw Viktor eyeing Elenna across the clearing. She stood beside Storm and Silver, her face creased with anxiety as she stretched her bowstring with an arrow. She shot at Viktor. He stood firm, and the shaft glanced harmlessly off the golden breastplate.

"My turn," hissed the knight, sheathing his sword.

He took his bow from his back and then reached over his shoulder. With a sickening snap, he took a golden arrow and placed it against the string.

Tom tried to stand, but sank back, his breath catching in his throat with horror. *I can't let my friend die…*

Viktor shot, and Elenna ducked, flattening herself to the ground. The arrow missed her by a fraction and buried itself in a tree, splitting the trunk. Storm stamped, and Silver stood his ground with his teeth bared.

"Lure Laus away!" called Tom, finally managing to stand. He wanted the Stag Beast as far from those arrows as possible. Viktor paused, as if unsure who to attack first. He took a step towards Elenna and Laus, reaching for another arrow. Tom saw

his chance and ran at the Deadly Archer. But instead of stabbing him, he slashed downwards with his sword, slicing through the clasps of the golden breastplate. It fell away from the Beast. Tom caught it, and ran to a safe distance. He fastened the breastplate over his own torso. Strength of heart surged through his chest.

"You'll need more than that to defeat me, *boy*," snarled Viktor, rounding on him.

Over Viktor's shoulder, Tom saw Elenna had sliced down a vine with her dagger and she was fashioning a lasso. She tossed it over Laus's ghostly antlers. The Beast reared up with hooves wheeling. Elenna strained at the other end of the rope, digging her heels into the ground.

*I have to keep Viktor distracted*, thought Tom. *She won't be able to hold on for long.*

He brandished his sword and slammed its blade three times against the face of his shield. "Soon you'll be back in your ice prison where you belong," said Tom.

Elenna was frantically tugging on Laus's antlers, but the Stag Beast strained against her.

"I'll never go back there," said Viktor. "Not while there are Beasts to hunt."

Laus tugged the rope free of Elenna's hands and she almost lost her footing. The two-headed stag turned on her with a bellow. Viktor spun around to look, drawing another arrow from his back. Tom threw himself at the Deadly Archer. His sword rang against the black leg-armour, sending up a shower of sparks, and the arrow twanged off from the string. Tom saw it score Laus's flank.

As Viktor stumbled backwards with a roar of anger, Tom attacked again. He thumped his sword-hilt against the horned helmet. Viktor's eyes rolled dizzily in his head and he toppled with a crash. To his right, Tom saw that Elenna had mounted Storm.

"Come and get me!" she shouted. With a thrust of his powerful haunches, Laus kicked after her

across the clearing, trailing blood
from his wound.

*Good idea, Elenna!* Tom thought.
*You'll lead him away from Viktor.*

But a horrible sharp yowl made
Elenna stop. Tom saw a grey
shape tossed into the air. As it hit
the ground again, he realised in

horror that it was Silver. He'd been trampled! Tom felt suddenly cold.

Elenna leapt from Storm's saddle and slapped his haunch to send him galloping away. She rushed to her wolf. Laus charged after Storm and they plunged into the trees. Tom raced towards his friend and Silver's motionless body. Time seemed to slow down. Was he… Could he be…

*Dead?*

Tom was almost at Elenna's side when he heard Viktor groan. From the corner of his eye, he saw the Deadly Archer rise. Then everything seemed to happen at once. Elenna looked up, her eyes filled with tears; Storm erupted from the trees behind her – Tom heard the twang of a bowstring. He caught the flash of gold – *an arrow!* – and hurled himself at Elenna, bundling her out of the way. The shaft thrummed past, slicing through the back of his tunic. Tom felt a sharp pain and hissed through his teeth.

He found himself lying beside Elenna on the ground. He reached back expecting to feel a golden arrow deep in his flesh. His fingers felt blood, but the scratch wasn't deep. Relief flooded through him as he stood gingerly. *The arrow must just have grazed my skin.*

Viktor stood erect, his bow clutched in his hands and a cruel smile playing on his lips. There was no sign of Laus.

*Perhaps he ran to safety...*

He faced the Deadly Archer. "You missed!" he said.

"No, I didn't," said Viktor. "Look behind you."

Elenna screamed, and Tom spun around. His breath left him in a groan of anguish. Storm was staggering weakly, the golden arrow lodged deep in his flank. His eyes rolled in fear. With a whinny of pain, his legs buckled and he fell sideways.

"No..." Tom muttered, sinking to his knees.

The Deadly Archer walked over to Storm's side and reached out for the arrow. As he touched it, Storm's body jerked on the ground, and the arrow disappeared. Viktor gave a happy sigh as Storm's soul travelled into his

body. His black armour shone even brighter than before.

"Your horse was strong," he said. "And now his strength is mine!" Viktor snapped another arrow free and aimed its point at Tom. "Your Quests are over…"

# STORY TWO

*Where are Tom and his friends? My instincts tell me that all is not well.*

*The Master of Arms lies in the infirmary. His eyes are like pale clouds. He lives, and yet he does not live. Can anything return his spirit to its home?*

*By candlelight I read the Annals of the Archers. It is not a happy story. I fear no Master of the Beasts – not even Tom – can defeat Viktor. It took all of the Wizard Circle to vanquish him before. And all Tom has are his courage and his sword.*

*The candle has gone out, snatched by an ill wind. I pray Tom's life will not be snuffed out as easily.*

*Yours, in gravest times,*

*Aduro, a wizard no more*

# ENTANGLED!

Tom felt a powerful shove to the shoulder and he fell. Viktor's golden arrow sped past Elenna's outstretched arms, striking a rotten tree stump.

As Tom scrambled to his feet, Viktor strode towards the arrow, then paused. Something was holding him back from retrieving his weapon.

Silver was whining softly on the ground. At least he was still alive.

From the depths of the forest came Laus's echoing cry. Viktor's head snapped around, and his eyes gleamed. Then he pointed a hand towards the bone-heap that had been his horse and barked, "Rise, Ossator!"

Before Tom's eyes, the bones began to reassemble themselves. Sockets and joints clicked into place, and the great curved ribs rose off the ground. Leg

bones shifted and locked, the creature stood again. It tossed its smooth white skull and snorted. The Deadly Archer mounted his stallion and turned to Tom and Elenna. "I've defeated your puny creatures. After I have taken Laus's power, I will come back for you too."

He gave Ossator's flank a vicious kick, and the skeleton horse stampeded across the clearing and into the trees.

"We must pursue the Beast," said Tom.

Elenna looked up from Silver's body, her eyes full of pain. Her glance travelled to Storm. "We can't leave them."

Tom felt a tug in his heart. *How can I desert our companions?* But he steeled himself. "If we don't fight Viktor, more innocent animals and Beasts will die."

Elenna stroked Silver's head. The wolf lifted his snout and licked her hand. She nodded. "I need you to stay here and look after Storm," she said, her voice thick. "Can you do that for me?" Silver whined, and tried to stand, but fell back again. "Brave boy. Lie still, for now."

She stood up, her face hard. "Viktor will pay for this," she said.

They set off after Viktor into the trees. Tom laid a hand on Storm's neck as they passed. His stallion was breathing, just as the Master of Arms had been, but his eyes were blank pools. "We'll come back for you and Silver," said Tom. "After we've made Viktor pay for what he has done."

They ran into the forest, following

Ossator's path of destruction through broken foliage and trampled leaves. Tom tried not to think about Storm lying in the clearing. *Perhaps there's something Daltec can do to bring back his soul.* Even as he hoped it, his heart sank. Daltec was young and inexperienced – he couldn't possibly handle magic so powerful.

Tom thought he heard breathing, so he paused. Elenna stopped too.

"What is it?" she whispered. Tom reached inside his tunic, and took out the parchment map.

"Viktor's that way," said Elenna urgently, pointing at a broken sapling and a patch of crushed ferns straight ahead.

Tom unfolded the map, and the

image of the forest sprang to life on its surface. Sure enough, the golden dot was moving quickly away from them. But a silver shape was edging nearer.

"Laus," Tom breathed. "He's close…"

With a snap of twigs, the Stag Beast burst from the trees on their left. He lowered his heads and charged. Tom drew his sword. As he leapt aside he brought his blade down on to the antlers, severing a whole branch.

Laus roared, his eyes flashing with anger as he skidded to a halt and turned in a tight circle. The vine lasso still dangled from the antlers that remained. Laus tossed his heads angrily then ran at Tom again. Tom leapt backwards as the dappled heads flashed past. Without thinking, Tom gripped the end of the trailing vine. Laus yanked him across the ground, but Tom managed to keep his feet. The Beast halted once more, and twisted to face them.

Tom's free hand went to the ruby jewel. *Don't attack*, he silently sent the message. *We're not your—*

Laus launched forwards, and Tom sprinted into the trees, still holding the vine. He ran in and out of the trunks, tangling the vine among them. He could hear Laus stamping after him, snorting with fury. Tom rounded a tree and doubled back, feeling gnarled roots slam into his shin. His body lurched forward as he tumbled to the ground. He rolled on to his back to see Laus coming right for him. As the Stag Beast reared up, hooves flashing, Tom shielded his face and prepared for pain.

But pain didn't come. Daring to look, he saw Laus straining against a lasso, the vine pulled taut behind him. He was trapped!

Tom scrambled out of harm's way, then drew his sword. Laus's eyes went wide. Tom rammed the blade, point

first, into the earth, then touched the jewel again. It was a risk. If Laus tore free, he'd trample Tom in an instant.

*We are not your enemies*, he said.

Laus's eyes blazed.

*We're here to protect you from a deadly hunter.*

Laus snorted and lunged at him, but the vine held tight. For now. The wound across his flank seeped blood.

Tom brought his shield around, and took off the talon which had once belonged to Epos.

*I can heal your wound*, he said.

The Stag Beast's eyes glittered with evil as he tore at the air with his hooves.

*Hear me, Laus*, said Tom. *I only mean to help you...*

Laus let his hooves drop, and his flanks heaved. Tom approached slowly, with the talon held at arm's length in front of him. Laus's black eyes watched him as he drew near, his teeth bared. Tom placed the talon carefully against the wound and willed it to work. All the time he was tense and ready to spring clear if Laus turned on him.

The cut under Laus's fur slowly sealed, and the blood dried and flaked away. Laus shuddered, then lowered his heads to the ground, and began to eat the plants there.

*You're safe here,* Tom said. *We'll be back soon.*

He retrieved his sword and saw Elenna watching him through the trees with an arrow ready.

Tom shook his head and walked over to join her.

"What now?" asked Elenna. "We need to find Viktor."

Tom rushed back through the trees to where the antlers lay on the path. A plan was forming in his mind. Perhaps he could use them to tempt Viktor into a fight.

He laid a hand on one of the curved branches. "I think the Deadly Archer will come to us," he said, "if he thinks we're Laus."

Elenna's eyes shone with pleasure. "Do you have a plan?" she asked.

Tom smiled. "Maybe. But it will involve fooling Viktor – and he may be too clever for us. If so, it's all over."

# BAITING THE BEAST

Tom checked the parchment map again. The Deadly Archer was moving steadily through the trees on the far side of the forest.

His eyes fell on the part where they'd almost stumbled into the stinking swamp. "I know just the place to lay a trap for Viktor!"

Tom hoisted up the antlers, which were lighter than they looked, and he and Elenna dashed through the forest towards the marsh. Tom kept the parchment map open in front of him, checking it regularly. He wasn't worried about being quiet now – he wanted Viktor to find them. Sure enough, the golden dot began to cross the forest in their direction. Tom only hoped that Laus remained out of the way. The trees grew closely packed as he and Elenna approached the swamp. The stench of the stagnant water soon filled Tom's nostrils. Giant misshapen toadstools grew at the base of trees, while poisonous mosses and bushes dotted the forest floor.

A hiss made them both duck. Less than a second later, a golden arrow sank into a patch of swamp grass.

Tom hurled the antlers into the middle of the marsh, and cried out: "Elenna, look! Laus is stuck in the swamp!"

He grabbed Elenna and tugged her behind a tree. A moment later, he heard the rattle of bones, and Ossator stepped into view. Viktor placed his fingers to the skeleton stallion's neck. "Sleep," he muttered. The horse collapsed into a pile of bones.

"Ha!" laughed the Deadly Archer. His armour gleamed. "This is easier than I expected." He looked around him. "I know you're here somewhere, boy!" Viktor snapped an arrow from his back, and aimed at the place where the antlers were sticking up through the marshy water. "Watch while I take Laus's soul and make it my own."

He fired an arrow into the murky water. The antlers didn't move. Tom peered out and saw Viktor frowning as he nocked a second arrow.

"It's working," Tom whispered to Elenna, but when he turned around, his friend had disappeared. Had she

gone back to Silver, when he needed her the most?

Viktor shot his second arrow. Again, the shaft disappeared into the water without a trace.

Tom drew his sword silently. *If I have to fight the Deadly Archer by myself, so be it.*

As Viktor strung a third arrow, the sound of Laus's bellowing call echoed through the midnight forest. Viktor lowered his bow. "I've been fooled…" he muttered. "Ossator – rise!"

The skeleton horse's frame began to reassemble, as though an invisible sculptor was re-forming the Beast. Before it was done, Tom saw a shape run from the trees behind Viktor.

*Elenna!*

Tom's friend hurled herself towards Viktor, swinging a rotten branch which smashed into the side of his head and knocked him into the putrid pond. The Beast's body sank beneath the green slime and bubbling water. He came up thrashing and choking, reaching for the

bank with his muscular arms.

*He can't swim!* Tom realised.

With a strangled cry, Viktor disappeared under the scummy surface. Tom rushed over to Elenna's side and stared into the marsh. Ossator was looking sadly over the bank, then backed away, snapping his bare teeth at them. As his fore-hooves reared, Elenna shot an arrow. It slammed straight through the horse's empty eye socket and into the tree behind, pinning the horrible stallion in place. With a rattle of bony joints, the creature tried to free itself but could not. After straining a few more moments, it sagged back against the trunk, defeated.

The murky surface of the swamp was still, apart from a few bubbles.

"You did it!" said Tom, clapping his friend on the back. "Laus is safe."

Elenna grimaced. "That was for Silver," she said.

Tom could hardly believe it was over. Normally he was the one who vanquished the Beasts. *Elenna deserves the glory*, he thought.

Now they had to get Storm back to the castle, to see if there was anything that could be done. And Silver would need treatment too.

"Our fight is done here," he said. "Let's see to the animals."

As they turned from the bank, Ossator's bony ears pricked up. Tom heard a rush of water and an angry roar. He spun around to see Viktor rising from the water, slime and weeds trailing from his armour.

"Come back here, boy!" the Beast bellowed, levelling his bow.

In three strides, Tom reached the marsh's edge, then he leapt at Viktor. He crashed into the Beast, knocking his arrow off-target.

The water swallowed them both.

# 3

# BENEATH THE FOREST

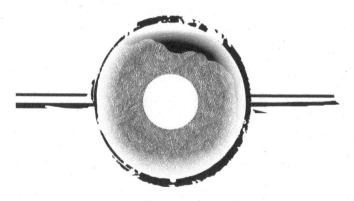

Tom could barely see as they wrestled in the swamp. He mistakenly gulped a mouthful of the disgusting pond-water and spat it out. Viktor was strong, but Tom had the Golden Breastplate. He aimed a punch at the Beast's head, but the water was so thick the blow had little power. Viktor's hand slipped around his throat and squeezed.

Black spots leapt up behind Tom's eyes. Viktor pressed him against the bottom of the pond. Tom scrabbled to draw his sword. With a stab, he forced the blade into the gap in Viktor's leg armour. A stream of bubbles burst from the Beast's mouth as he roared in pain and released his grip on Tom's neck.

Tom tried to stand, but his feet just sank into the foul mud. He could not last much longer. As he tried to kick to the surface, he realised his feet were stuck. He writhed and yanked his legs, and felt the boggy ground shift a little. More bubbles rose from the ground, as if another crack had opened up below.

Tom was close to blacking out
when a shape sank through the water
beside him. It was Viktor, holding an
arrow in one hand but no bow. He
floated in front of Tom, then raised
the arrow so the point hovered over
Tom's heart. Viktor was grinning

wildly. He reached with his empty hand and touched the ruby at Tom's waist. His voice travelled into Tom's brain, taunting him:

*Your soul is mine, Master of the Beasts!*

Tom heaved at his legs as he felt the arrow point press against his tunic. He wondered what it would be like, to feel his strength sucked away. How much would it hurt? The arrow point broke his skin. Tom clenched his teeth as he struggled to loosen the mud's grip. Spent breath scorched his lungs. His legs pulled free, and suddenly the ground all around him began to collapse.

He was falling. They both were. Viktor's eyes went wide with fear, as they tumbled through the hole that opened up beneath them. Tom's world spun around and around as he fell headlong in a flurry of stinking mud. He slid to a halt, soaked through and covered in slime. He gasped huge breaths. *I'm alive!*

Gradually his eyes adjusted to the gloom. He found himself lying on his back in some sort of cavern. Above was a slope of slick mud leading up to a patch of torn ground. Through the hole, he could see the distant glow of the moon. Gnarled tree roots like giant white worms broke through the roof and hung in empty space. *Underground?* The bottom of the pond had been just a thin layer above this world.

But where was Viktor?

Tom stood shakily, checking he still had his sword and shield. The intense heat reminded him of the crater of Stonewin volcano. Sweat prickled across his skin. He heard the clank of armour plates. A few paces away, Viktor was heaving himself out of the mud too. He spat out a mouthful of swamp water, and glared at Tom.

"You tricked me," he said. "Laus was never in that swamp."

"That's right," said Tom, drawing his sword. "And the only way you'll leave this place is over my dead body."

Viktor narrowed his eyes and took an arrow from his back. "That can be arranged."

Tom leapt back and the arrow

slammed into the ground at his feet. He ran further into the cavern, ducking beneath more trailing vegetation. Sweat poured off his head onto his already sodden clothes.

"Come back here, you coward!" snarled Viktor. Another arrow shot past Tom's ear and buried itself in the dense black mud and rotten leaves of the cavern wall.

Some of the snaking tendrils were thicker than a man's waist, and reached right from the ceiling to the floor. The air was like a hot soup.

Tom hid behind a root and peeked out to see Viktor stalking after him, bow swaying from side to side. He only had three more arrows bristling from his back. He placed one to his bowstring. "No one escapes the Deadly Archer!" he said.

"And evil does not escape the Master of the Beasts," Tom replied.

Viktor jerked around and loosed the arrow. It slammed through the root beside Tom, its golden point bursting through the far side.

Two arrows left. *If I can just get him to lose the last of his weapons...*

Tom rushed from one tree root to the next, and another arrow flashed like lightning through the gloom. Tom ducked and it sliced through the air above his head.

"My friend Elenna is a better shot than you," Tom taunted.

With a roar of intent, Viktor loosed his final arrow.

Tom raised his shield and braced himself. The shaft skimmed off the wood and shot into the darkness.

"Looks like you're out of arrows," said Tom.

Viktor snorted. "I still have this!" He drew his huge broadsword, and

swung it over his head. With a mighty sweep, he severed a trunk-sized root. "You're next," he called to Tom.

Tom stepped out from his hiding place and drew his sword. His palm was slippery around the hilt. "We'll see about that!"

Something tickled Tom's leg and he looked down to see a beetle the size of his fist crawling over his ankle. *Urgh!* He brushed it away, but more were climbing over his feet. Now he looked closer he saw other creatures scurrying across the ground – giant centipedes, translucent worms, and lice glowing white with black beating hearts pulsing under their skin. He heard heavy footsteps and raised his sword as Viktor attacked. The ringing blow sent Tom reeling into a tree root, and tore his sword out of his hand. Pain lanced through Tom's wrist and elbow. Sweat trickled into his eyes and he blinked it away.

Viktor swung again and Tom ducked as his enemy's blade sliced into the cavern wall. He saw his chance and rolled beneath the Beast's legs. Where was his sword? As Viktor tried to free his weapon, Tom leapt on to the Deadly Archer's back, gripping the horns of his helmet with both hands.

At once, a strange invisible fire crept across his hands and over his wrists. But it was not a painful fire. It felt more like...*power*.

Viktor roared with rage and tried to

reach up to Tom with his gauntleted fists. But his thick plates of armour wouldn't let him. He staggered sideways, shaking his head. Tom hung on grimly, his anger growing with every heaving breath he took. He wanted to twist Viktor's head right off his shoulders.

He wanted to hurt this Beast and relish his pain.

*What's happening to me?* Tom wondered. Hatred seemed to swell through his veins, clouding his heart. Fury had replaced any sense of honour.

*Am I becoming evil?*

# 4

# CHANNELLING EVIL

With one hand still clutching the Beast's horned helmet, Tom managed to slip an arm around Viktor's neck and squeeze. The Beast thrashed, but couldn't escape.

"While there's blood in my veins, I'll kill you!" Tom roared, as Viktor fell to one knee, his breath rasping. Tom felt like he was watching himself from a distance as he wrung the Beast's life away. In a vision, he saw his own face, twisted with fury and malice, his eyes bloodshot and raging.

*What am I doing? This isn't the hero's way…*

Never before had he taken the life of a Beast at his mercy.

*Stop!* he told himself.

A low rattle escaped Viktor's throat.

*This isn't right!*

Tom released his hold and jumped clear. At once, the blackness over his heart lifted. Viktor was choking as he crawled towards the wall where his sword was still lodged.

*It must have been his helmet,* Tom realised. *The Beast's evil was infecting me.*

Viktor found his feet again, and seized his sword from the wall. As he turned to Tom, his teeth were bared.

Tom saw his own sword in the thick mud. "Give up," he told the Beast. "I've shown you mercy."

The Deadly Archer grinned as he stamped forward, snatching up his spent arrows. "Then you're a fool," he said. "You should have killed me while you had the chance."

With four arrows intact once more, he stood tall and proud.

*I don't know how much longer I can last*, Tom thought.

Viktor strode towards him and Tom backed away, feeling the cavern wall at his back. There was nowhere to run.

As the Deadly Archer took aim, his eyes suddenly shifted, staring beyond his prey. Tom turned and saw Elenna fire an arrow which glanced off Viktor's shoulder. He staggered backwards with a cry.

"Elenna!" Tom cried. "Stay back."

If his friend heard him, she didn't listen. She was scrambling down the slope of mud from the collapsed pond. She shot another arrow, which stabbed the ground at Viktor's feet.

"I couldn't leave all the fun to you," she called.

Viktor sent a golden arrow her way. Elenna somersaulted nimbly over it and replied with a shot of her own. The Beast tried to duck, but the arrow dislodged his helmet with a sucking noise. The Deadly Archer hissed with anger and Tom gasped when he saw the Beast's exposed face.

It was like a rotten fruit left too long in the sun, the skin blackened and wrinkled. Despite everything, Tom felt a twinge of pity.

"Pretty, aren't I?" snarled the Deadly Archer, before he dropped to a crouch and aimed another arrow. Elenna sheltered behind a tree root.

Tom's eyes fell on the Beast's fallen helmet. The thrill of its power still tingled in his limbs. He wondered, could he wear it himself? Could he control the evil impulse that would surely rage through him?

If he managed to use its power, it might be enough to defeat Viktor.

The Beast was stalking towards his friend. As Elenna tried to line up another arrow, Viktor seized her by the hair and raised her in front of him with one powerful arm. Elenna twisted and screamed in his grasp, trying to free herself with wild kicks.

Viktor drew his sword slowly, as if he was savouring the moment.

*I don't have a choice*, thought Tom. He looked again at the helmet. *If I don't use this, he will kill Elenna…*

He snatched up the helmet and put it on. Anger flooded through Tom's veins like fire. It felt good.

"Viktor!" he shouted, staring down his sword. "Prepare to be defeated!"

# 5

# THE POWER OF DARKNESS

Viktor's shrivelled features turned to face Tom and a low growl emerged from his throat. With a jerk of his arm, he threw Elenna viciously aside. Tom winced as his friend crashed into the cavern wall and lay still. Another rush of fury hit him. With a roar from the depths of his belly, he charged at the Deadly Archer.

As Tom raised his sword above his head, Viktor swung his blade. The metal clashed with a bone-shaking *clang* that set Tom's ears ringing. He hacked again, and again Viktor parried before aiming a kick that sent Tom sprawling through the mud on his back. His eyes searched for Elenna,

but she was gone.

*Typical!* he thought, his anger swelling again. *What a cowardly, pathetic girl!*

Viktor sprang at him, sword held in both hands with the point facing downwards – towards Tom's heart.

Tom rolled sideways as the massive blade sank into the ground where he'd been lying. He found his feet again, but the heat and the weight of the helmet, combined with the waves of fury and hate, were making the world spin all around him.

Facing the Beast, Tom imagined driving his sword through his enemy's heart. He longed to look into Viktor's eyes as he snatched his life away. He wanted to taste the Beast's pain.

Viktor's chest was heaving with rasping breaths. *He's fading,* Tom thought. *He won't last much longer.*

Tom ran at the Beast, and feinted with his sword towards Viktor's leg. As Viktor twisted to dodge the low blow, Tom drove his shield against the side of the Deadly Archer's unprotected head and sent him reeling. Viktor fell heavily on to his back into the mud. Tom laid his foot on the Beast's chest and pressed his sword point against his neck.

The Deadly Archer stared at him, his eyes heavy with defeat. "Please!" he said. "Don't kill me!"

"What are you doing, Tom?" called Elenna.

Tom saw his friend standing on the

mud slope.

"Stay out of this!" Tom shouted. "He belongs to me!"

Keeping the pressure on his sword hilt, he leant over the Beast and pulled away his golden bow with his free hand. With three powerful strikes, Tom smashed it to splinters against the ground.

"I'm at your mercy now," said the Beast. "Victory is yours."

"Not yet, it isn't," Tom snarled. "You're still alive."

"But you're a Master of the Beasts," said Viktor, his sunken eyes widening. "You can't…"

Tom leant more heavily on his sword. Blood began to ooze from Viktor's wound. *I'm going to enjoy this…*

"OOOF!"

Tom lost his footing as a blow hit him on the side of the head. He rolled over as the Beast's helmet fell off. He righted himself and looked up. Elenna was standing there, her bow held in her hands like a club. Viktor sagged back in the mud, letting out a

gasp of relief.

"Tom," said Elenna, her face creased with a puzzled frown. "What's happened to you?"

Tom shook his head, then stared at the discarded helmet. "I thought I could control Viktor's evil power."

Shame burned within him, but already he felt the pall of evil disappearing. "Thank you, Elenna. You saved me from myself."

"Turn to starboard!"

They both looked up at the sound of a gruff voice. Through the broken ground above, Tom saw a dark shape pass through the night sky.

Elenna gasped. "Sanpao's ship!"

Then Kensa's screeching voice drifted down too. "I see Laus!" she called. "Oh my, he's tied up already. His antlers will look very nice on my workshop wall. It's time to go Beast-hunting!"

Elenna's fear-filled eyes met Tom's.

"Go after them, Elenna!" Tom yelled. "Save Laus!"

Elenna nodded and sprinted up the slope to the open air, slipping and sliding over the mud. As she disappeared over the lip of the hole, the ground shifted, and more of the pond began to collapse into the cavern.

Tom's eyes fell upon Viktor. The Deadly Archer was looking at him desperately. "Good Master of the Beasts," he said, his shrivelled lips trembling. "Do not leave me!"

# 6

# SHIPWRECK

The cavern walls were shaking, and huge clots of black mud broke free and toppled to the ground. It would not be long before the whole place collapsed and buried them alive.

Staring into the Beast's pathetic face, Tom couldn't believe he had been so ready to murder the Deadly Archer. *I can't abandon him to die here.*

He reached out a hand, and Viktor

raised his arm. As their palms touched, pain seared through Tom's skin. A cruel smile broke over Viktor's wizened features as he pulled Tom closer to him.

"We shall both die down here!" the Beast cackled.

Blood leaked from between their hands, and Tom realised that the Beast's gauntlet was covered in dozens of tiny barbs, almost too small to see. Even now, in the throes of death, the Deadly Archer was consumed by evil intentions.

"I tried to help you," Tom said, struggling to free himself. His hand thrummed with pain, as if stung by a hundred bees.

"Then you're a fool," said Viktor.

"I've killed one Master of the Beasts already. Your end will make my own more bearable!"

"But we could both live!" said Tom.

Viktor's face was filled with hatred. "Not this time," he snarled.

A sound like a waterfall made Tom turn. His heart contracted as he saw a huge section of the cavern roof turn to liquid. A muddy torrent crashed into them. Tom craned his neck to keep his head above the deluge as it swallowed Viktor's body whole. As mud spattered his face, Tom looked down and saw that Viktor was completely submerged. Only his mighty arm, still clutching Tom's hand, poked through. The Beast was drowning in the slick of clotted mud.

*There is no way to free him now*, Tom told himself.

Gradually, the Deadly Archer's grip weakened, and his fingers went limp. Tom prised his bleeding hand free.

"What a horrible end..." he muttered.

It took what remained of Tom's

strength to drag himself free of the
mud. He found his sword hilt sticking
up a few paces away and yanked it
from the swamp's clutches.

Breathing heavily, he looked up
through the gash in the earth's
surface. There wasn't time to rest. He
had to find Elenna.

*There's one more battle to face...*

With his clothes pasted in filth, Tom
clambered out into the open air. The
moonlight fell upon a cluster of bones
beside a tree. Ossator's skull still
dangled from Elenna's arrow, but the
rest of the skeleton horse had fallen
to pieces.

*He doesn't have any purpose now.*

Tom pulled out the arrow, and laid
the bones one by one into the hole.
*They should rest together*, he thought.
*Rider and steed.*

At the sound of hooves, panic rose
in Tom's heart. A moment later, a
shape burst through the trees. It took
him a heartbeat to understand what
he was seeing – Elenna's smiling face
cast in the glow of majestic silver
antlers. She sat astride the Beast of

the forest, the trailing vine forming
makeshift reins. Magically, Laus's
antlers seemed to have re-formed.

"How did you—"Tom began.

Elenna grinned again. "Laus doesn't
seem to be evil any more," she said.

Laus tossed his two heads and bellowed with joy. *The Beast must have realised we're his friends*, Tom thought. *We've taken away the only one who could harm him.*

"Viktor?" Elenna asked.

Tom shook his head. "Buried forever," he said. "But where are Kensa and Sanpao?"

Elenna glanced back into the forest. "They're on my tail, somewhere…"

As she spoke, Tom heard the snap and crash of splintering branches.

"I'm telling you," bellowed Sanpao, "they came this way."

"We're too low, fish-breath!" screeched Kensa. "We need to climb!"

The prow of the ship broke above the trees, red sails flying.

"There she is!" roared Sanpao, pointing. "Lower!"

The ship lurched downwards, and the Pirate King leaned over the rail. In his hands was a giant crossbow made of bones. "Venison stew for supper, me hearties!" he shouted.

Kensa flew across the deck. "We're going to crash!"

The vessel crunched into a tree trunk, and tilted sideways. Sanpao was thrown backwards out of sight. The whole ship turned on to its side and its masts broke as they caught the ground. The terrified cries of the crew filled the air.

With a sucking sound, Sanpao's ship smacked into the stinking pond, throwing up a wave of filthy water.

Timbers creaked as the huge vessel settled into the marsh. Then a voice broke the silence. "What did I tell you?" said Kensa. "I've met shellfish with more brains than you!"

"I almost had them," moaned Sanpao.

Tom turned to Elenna with a grin. "It'll take them a while to get ship-shape again," he said.

Elenna returned his smile, but her look of happiness faded quickly. "Let's get back to Storm and Silver," she said. "Jump on."

Tom approached Laus slowly, the Beast's two sets of eyes watching him.

"It's quite safe," said Elenna.

Tom had to stand on a tree stump to climb Laus's broad back. Elenna gave the reins a gentle tug, and nudged the Beast's sides with her foot. The two-headed stag galloped off into the forest, back towards the clearing. Any sense of exhilaration left Tom at once when he saw Storm's black form lying motionless in the broken foliage.

*We're too late*, he thought, grief seizing him. *My brave horse is dead.*

# 7

# THE BREATH OF LIFE

Silver lifted his grey head as they grew nearer. He climbed weakly to his paws and growled through bared teeth.

"It's all right," soothed Elenna. "Laus is our ally now."

Silver sank down beside Storm's body again, and Tom slipped off the Beast's back. With dread in his slow

steps, he reached Storm's side and
fell to his knees. Tears pricked at his
eyes as he laid an ear against the
horse's cold flank. There was no hint
of a breath, and not even the slightest
beating of his stallion's brave heart.
He felt Elenna's hand on his shoulder.

*He shouldn't have died,* Tom thought. *I should have saved him, as he's saved me so many times. No Quest is worth this.*

The skin beneath his cheek trembled. Tom looked up, and saw that Laus had lowered one of his heads. He was touching his muzzle to Storm's nose and his silver antlers were glowing brighter than ever. A fine silver mist, like sparkling steam, flowed from his nose and seeped into Storm's nostrils.

"What's he doing?" Elenna whispered.

A thin whinny broke through the cloud of Tom's grief, and Storm's eyes fluttered open. They were no longer blank, but back to their rich mahogany. Laus backed away as Storm staggered to his feet and tossed his head. Under the moonlight, his coat shone like polished jet. Silver tipped back his head and howled, obviously glad to see his old companion alive and well again.

Tom leapt up and threw his arms around his stallion's neck, burying his head in his glossy mane.

"That must be why Viktor wanted to kill Laus," said Elenna. "Laus has the power to restore the Deadly Archer's victims."

"Then we should thank him," said Tom. But when he turned around, the two-headed stag had disappeared. The trees were rustling on the far side of the clearing. "I suppose he wants to remain a mystery," said Tom. "Come on, let's go back to the palace and get Silver some help too."

"I think I can help with that," said a voice.

Daltec was sitting on a tree trunk a few paces away, his outline slightly blurred. "Do not worry for Laus," he said. "He will return again next year. Now, let's take you home."

Silver yapped, and Daltec held out both hands. His lips moved in a spell, and the forest around them began to vanish.

Tom found himself back in the palace courtyard with his friends. The first pink fingers of dawn were spreading across from the horizon. Elenna knelt beside Silver and gingerly ran her fingers over his fur.

Silver whined. "It's a couple of broken ribs," she said. "I can find some herbs to help the bones knit, but really he just needs to rest."

Daltec and Aduro stood beside one another smiling. "There's someone you should see," said the old man. He stood aside. Behind him, looking pale but unhurt, was the Master of Arms. His eyes too had returned to their normal blue.

"I had the strangest dream," he said, rubbing his head. "A stag was standing over me, and he was breathing silver clouds! When I woke up, I was in the infirmary. What's going on?"

Tom laughed. "It's a long story, my friend."

Daltec held out the copy of the *Annals of the Archers*. "You could read this," he said.

The Master of Arms took the book with a frown.

"I sense that Viktor won't trouble Avantia again," said Aduro.

Tom let his gaze settle on the ground. "I tried to rescue him," he

said, "but he refused to turn away from evil."

Aduro nodded gravely. "Some Beasts cannot be saved."

"Speaking of evil," Elenna said. "I wonder if Sanpao and Kensa have managed to get airborne again."

"They're probably still squabbling!" replied Tom.

Elenna laughed then wrinkled her nose. "Hopefully there'll be time for a bath before they're ready to threaten us again."

Tom grinned at her. "That's the best idea I've heard for a while," he said. "Fear not. If they return to Avantia, they will have us to deal with. Like always."

THE END

# CONGRATULATIONS, YOU HAVE COMPLETED THIS QUEST!

At the end of each chapter you were awarded a special gold coin.
The QUEST in this book was worth an amazing 14 coins.

Look at the Beast Quest totem picture inside the back cover of this book to see how far you've come in your journey to become

MASTER OF THE BEASTS.

The more books you read, the more coins you will collect!

Do you want your own
Beast Quest Totem?

1. Cut out and collect the coin below
2. Go to the Beast Quest website
3. Download and print out your totem
4. Add your coin to the totem
www.beastquest.co.uk/totem

*Have you read the latest series of Beast Quest? Read on for a sneak peek at KRYTOR THE BLOOD BAT!*

## CHAPTER ONE

## HOME!

"Ouch!" Elenna yelped, hopping on to one foot. "I've got a stone in my boot!"

Tom grinned as he watched his friend retrieve the stone and hurl it away.

"Just a little pebble," he said, pleased to have a moment to rest. "I can't believe you're complaining so much. We've been through worse."

"A lot worse." Elenna laughed. "Why couldn't Daltec magic us back from Gwildor?"

*She has a point*, Tom thought. The journey back to Avantia had been long and gruelling, taking them over both land and sea.

Tom lifted his chin. Being a Master of Beasts meant doing difficult things. This journey home was just part of that. He pointed up ahead at the soaring towers of King Hugo's palace in the City. "Look, not that far now."

*Read KRYTOR THE BLOOD BAT*
*to find out more!*

# Fight the Beasts,
# Fear the Magic

Do you want to know more
about BEAST QUEST?
Then join our Quest Club!

Visit
www.beastquest.co.uk/club
and sign up today!

Are you a collector of the Beast Quest Cards?
Visit the website for further information.